MW00878155

Purpose: The purpose of this book is to provide basic reading for children ages 1 and up. Please feel free to contact me at littleyapperbooks@gmail.com for comments.

About the author: Jane is an author, designer and educator. These days, you will find her drawing and writing children's books. She draws her inspiration from her students and her daughter. Jane lives in the Big Apple with her husband, daughter and beloved yorkies.

Author Page: www.amazon.com/author/janethai

Dedication: In memory of Forrest & Mocha Lee

I belong to:

Author's Notes

Help your child begin and build their first words in Chinese. This easy to follow picture word book is written in both English and simplified Chinese. Children learn best with visuals and can be taught to be bilingual at a very young age. In fact it is recommended that they learn another language as early as possible. This book contains many everyday objects and animals that children will see. Help your child reinforce vocabulary by pointing to real life objects at home or anywhere else. If you do not speak Chinese, you can still teach your child and give them a starting foundation to work with. Audio files of this book can be downloaded free with purchase of book at littleyapper.com. Have fun learning together!

Learn more about how to teach your child a second language at littleyapper.com.

LIVE & LEARN

FIRST WORDS IN CHINESE

中文 的 第一批词语
zhōngwén de dì yī pī cí yǔ

Numbers

数字
shùzì

1 一
yī

2 二
èr

3 三
sān

4 四
sì

5 五
wǔ

Bobby Big Foot

Written by Alex Niven
Illustrated by Eduardo Paj

Bobby Bigfoot

Written by Alex Niven
Illustrated by Eduardo Paj

I dedicate this book to my family who has supported me along the way and never allowed me to give up on my dream.
To my boys Neil and Journey, I love you with all my heart.
My wife Rachael, who was a big inspiration to this story.
My step father Bobby, who has always taken care of me like I was his own.
My mother Lori, someone who told me to never quit on my dreams.
My grandmother Carol, one of my biggest supporters since the beginning.
My father-in-law Ken and Kevin, you'll both be greatly missed.
To my illustrator Eduardo, who absolutely took my characters
and story and brought them to life.
To all my family and friends that I forgot to mention . Thank you all.

The morning of April 3rd starts off like any other morning
for Bobby Bigfoot. With Bobby getting ready to go on his
daily walk through the woods.
He sits on his log chair reading the Forest Spotter paper.

On the front page he sees that someone took a picture
of his neighbor Lori Littlefoot.
He has never had his picture taken by a human
and that is something he is very proud of.

Bobby gets up to start his day and says bye to his pet fox,
then heads out of his cave.

Today Bobby decides to walk along the river looking at the wildlife. He's been walking for hours and his stomach made a loud grumbling sound, RUMBLE GRUMBLE! He realizes he is getting hungry. He knew that there was a near by berry patch and starts heading down the path.

He walks into the clearing, sees all the colorful berries.
Without hesitating he starts grabbing handfulls of them
and starts shoving them in his mouth.
Then all of a sudden he hears a crackle sound, CRUNCH!
He starts looking up slowly..... CLICK!!!

He see's a little girl with a camera just standing feet away. He was so hungry that he didnt even look around to make sure he was alone.
At that moment he realizes, that someone just took the closest picture anyone has ever taken.

Shocked. He growled "RAAAAAWR!" The little girl just looked up at him and giggled. Bobby blurted out, "Am I not scary?"
Realizing that he just spoke to a human.

The little girl just took the photo
and started shaking it and looked up
at Bobby and replied,
"You dont look that scary."
Bobby was surprised that she didnt
run off like everyone else.

He knew the nearest place was a campground
and it's more than a days walk.
"Why are you out here all alone," he asked?
"I was camping with with my mom and stepdad,
and he wanted me to come inside early.
I got mad and ran away," she replied.

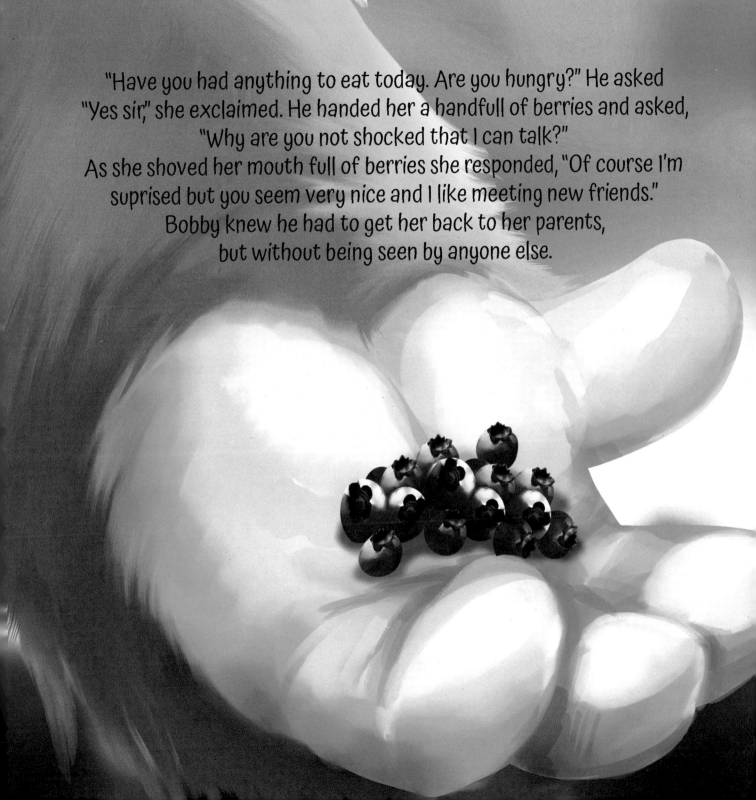

"Have you had anything to eat today. Are you hungry?" He asked
"Yes sir," she exclaimed. He handed her a handfull of berries and asked,
"Why are you not shocked that I can talk?"
As she shoved her mouth full of berries she responded, "Of course I'm
suprised but you seem very nice and I like meeting new friends."
Bobby knew he had to get her back to her parents,
but without being seen by anyone else.

As the little girl kept eating she asked, "What kind of berries are these?'
'Oh! They are blueberries, rasberries and blackberries," he replied.
"They are good, real good," she said.
"Whats your name?", Bobby asked.
"My name is Rachael, whats yours?"
"My name is Bobby, Bobby Bigfoot and it's nice to meet you Rachael."

Rachael asked, "What are you doing out here?"
"Im headed down the river today, want to come along?" he asked.
"Anywhere but back with my parents," she replied.
Bobby knew she had to go home but it was nice talking
to someone once in while.

She grabbed her camera and started to catch up to Bobby.
She giggled, "You know, you dont look half bad in this photo."
Bobby chuckled.

"Why do you have a camera?" Bobby asked.
"I love taking photos of the wildlife," she replied.
After walking for a few hours and making small talk. It was starting to get late. Bobby found a small over hang on the side of the cliff.
"Here!" said Bobby. "We'll sleep here for the night." As Bobby was building a shelter with some fallen tree limbs.

A tiny spider landed on Bobby's nose. He started freaking out and jumping up and down. "GET IT OFF, GET IT OFF!" Bobby cried! Rachael couldn't control her laughter but mananged to stop for a few seconds and grabbed a stick and said, "Stay still, let me get him."

Bobby tried his best not to move and Rachael slowly got the spider off his nose. "How is someone as BIG as you, so scared of a little spider?" "Because they have too many eyes," he cried. Rachael just couldn't help to let out a laugh.

Things finally calmed down for Bobby and they just laid there,
staring up at the stars.
Rachael asked, "Are you the only bigfoot?
Are you the one people keep taking pictures of?"
"Up until you, I have never had my picture taken,
and thats my neighbor Lori, who keeps getting caught, "Bobby replied.

"What's she like?" Rachael quickly asked.
"Oh, there is so much I could say about Lori Littlefoot.
She's so beautiful, oops! I mean, no more questions.
Its time for bed," Bobby said in a snap.
"Alright, goodnight Bobby, See you in the morning. She sounds like a keeper
by the way," she giggled as she started to fall asleep on Bobby's arm.
The night went on as Bobby watched over Rachael sleeping.

The warm sun started to shine through the trees the next morning.
Bobby had already gotten up to find some breakfast for them both.
Bobby brought a huge leaf full of different kind of figs and berries.
"Good morning," whispered Bobby. Rachael woke up
and started sniffing the air. "SNIFF, SNIFF, That smells good," she said!

Bobby let Rachael eat breakfast and said,
"We need to get going, got a lot more places to see."
They walked a little ways, looking at the squirels
and rabbits. Passing a beautiful waterfall.
As they walked along the trail near the river,
Bobby can see a look out tower that watches over the
forest and he knows the ranger is normally there.
Maybe he can take Rachael back to her parents.

Bobby asked, "Don't you want to see your parents again?"
"No! My stepdad was mean to me," she yelled!
"He wasn't being mean, maybe you're not making it easy for him,"
Bobby explained.
"I guess you're right Bobby. I just wanted to play with my new
friends. I don't have any back home.
Maybe I should have listened to him," she cried
"I know you did, but you know they love you and are very worried
about you right now, and I have an idea to get you home."

"Before I go home, can I give you something?" she asked.
"Of course you can," he replied.
"I want to give you something to always remember me by," she said.
It was a photo she took earlier of herself.

She handed it to Bobby with a smile. "You have been my best friend,"
she said in a sadden tone. "Can I keep the photo of you if I promise to never
show anyone?" Rachael asked.

Bobby looked at Rachael
and knew then she would never do
that and said,
"I would love for you to keep it."

As they got closer to the ranger tower. Bobby looked at Rachael
with a sad look and said, "Im going to miss you but I promise,
you'll make plenty of friends if you just be yourself."
He leaned down to give her a hug.
"Im going to always remember you Bobby," she cried.

Rachael walked out of the woods and within a few feet the park ranger started running down the stairs.
"RACHAEL," the ranger yelled! As he ran up to her with excitement.
"Where have you been, your parents are worried sick about you?" he asked.
"I walked along the river and seen the tower," she replied.
"Lets get you home," he said with a sigh of relief.

They hopped into the rangers truck and headed down the dirt trail
towards the campground.
"Im glad your safe and sound," the ranger said.
As they pulled into the campground and seen a crowd of people gathered
around to go out and do another search.

Rachael saw her parents. As soon as the truck stopped, she jumped out and
ran straight to them.
"MOM! DAD! I'm so sorry I ran away," she cried
as she jumped up to hug them both.
"Rachael, it doesn't matter, were just glad you're safe,"
her mom said with tears of joy.

Her stepdad looked up at the ranger, "How can we ever thank you enough,
Ranger Green?" "Its my job to always look
after the people and animals in the forest,"
he replied.

Ranger Green leaned down and whispered to Rachael,
"I'm glad you are safe, I'll tell Bobby you made it home ok."
With a confused look on her face she asked,
"How did you know about Bobby?"
Ranger Green replied, "A few years ago, my 2 grandsons wondered off
from the tower and Bobby found them and brought them back to me.
I've watched over him and the others.
"Theres more than 2?" Rachael asked.
"There's one out there, that always seems to be getting her photo taken,"
he said.
"That must be Lori Littlefoot, Bobby mentioned her," she replied.
"I wish I got to see the others. Maybe one day, but I got to go!
Thank you so much for taking me back Ranger Green," she said.

As Rachael walked back with her parents to the camper, she stopped and looked out at the forest and pulled out the photo of Bobby. She whispered to herself, "Thank you Bobby Bigfoot, I'll always remember you."

From a distance up on the hill, Bobby looks out over the campground, while holding the photo of Rachael. He says to himself, "You'll always be my bestfriend."

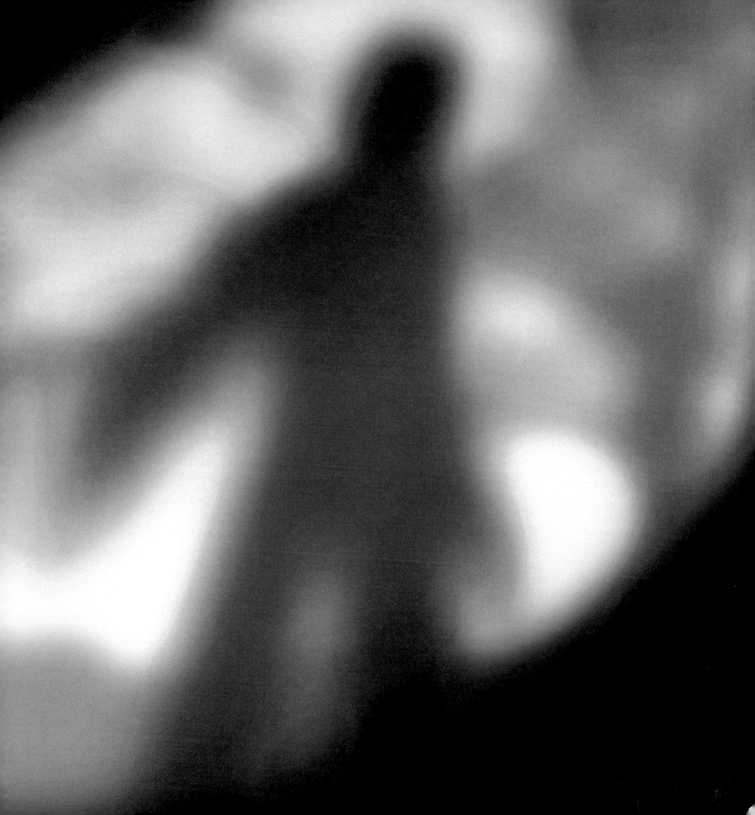

Bobby turned around when he heard crunching sounds
behind him: CRUNCH! CRUNCH! CRUNCH! CRUNCH!

Bobby realized it was footsteps headed straight
for him, and he had no place to hide.
He got so scared that as he took a step backwards;
he tripped and bumped his head.
As he opened his eyes, he saw a shadowy figure
getting closer. He then heard, "Bobby?"

TO BE CONTINUED...

Made in the USA
Las Vegas, NV
14 August 2021